Coco
the Cupcake
Fairy

Special thanks to
Rachel Elliot

ORCHARD BOOKS
338 Euston Road, London NW1 3BH
Orchard Books Australia
Level 17/207 Kent Street, Sydney, NSW 2000
A Paperback Original

First published in 2013 by Orchard Books

HiT entertainment

A CIP catalogue record for this book is available
from the British Library.

ISBN 978 1 40832 498 1

3 5 7 9 10 8 6 4

Printed in Great Britain

The paper and board used in this paperback are natural recyclable
products made from wood grown in sustainable forests. The
manufacturing processes conform to the environmental regulations
of the country of origin.

Orchard Books is a division of Hachette Children's Books,
an Hachette UK company

www.hachette.co.uk

Coco
the Cupcake
Fairy

by Daisy Meadows

ORCHARD

www.rainbowmagic.co.uk

The Fairyland Palace

Candy Land

Goblins' ice cream van

Market St

Charlie's ice cream

Kirsty's Hou

Wetherbury Village

Jack Frost's
Ice Castle

Funfair

The Park

Sweet
Shop

The High St.

Jack Frost's Spell

I have a plan to cause some strife
And use those fairies to change my life.
I'm going to take their charms away
And make my dreams come true today!

I'll build a castle made of sweets,
And spoil the fairies' silly treats.
I just don't care how much they whine,
Their cakes and lollies will be mine!

Contents

A Sweet Surprise

"This has been such an exciting day," said Rachel Walker, licking her Marshmallow Magic ice cream. "We've already been to Fairyland and helped two fairies get their magical objects back from Jack Frost."

Rachel and her best friend Kirsty Tate were walking home from the Wetherbury village square, where they had been looking around the market.

Rachel was visiting Kirsty for half term, and it looked as if they were going to have an exciting holiday.

"The day's not over yet," added Kirsty, smiling.

She paused to lick her Strawberry Sparkle ice cream, which was melting in the hazy afternoon sun and running over her fingers.

"I've got a feeling that now magical things have *started* happening, they're going to keep *on* happening!" she went on, licking her fingers one by one.

No one in the human world knew that

the girls had been on many adventures in Fairyland. They were always keen to make new fairy friends, and often they had to help outwit naughty Jack Frost and his troublesome goblin servants. That morning, Honey the Sweet Fairy had visited them to ask for their help. Jack Frost and his goblins had stolen the seven magical objects belonging to the Sweet Fairies. Without them, all the sweets in both the human world and Fairyland were being spoiled.

"We've already rescued Lottie the Lollipop Fairy's magical lollipop and Esme the Ice Cream Fairy's magical cone charms," remembered Rachel, chewing on a deliciously sticky marshmallow. "But there are still five more objects to find."

"And if we don't find them quickly, Treat Day will be ruined," said Kirsty.

The day after tomorrow was Treat Day in Fairyland. King Oberon and Queen Titania always gave a treat basket to each fairy. But Jack Frost was using the magical objects to get all the sweets for himself, so there weren't any left for the fairies. He was planning to build a giant Candy Castle, and he had given the magical charms to his goblins for safekeeping.

The goblins had come to the human world to find even *more* sweets for the Ice Lord's Candy Castle. Rachel and Kirsty kept a careful lookout for the little green troublemakers as they strolled past the village hall. They knew that goblins could pop up anywhere.

"It's not just magical things that we have to look forward to," Rachel reminded her friend. "It's nearly your birthday, and Aunt Harri said that she was going to have a surprise waiting for you at home, remember?"

Aunt Harri had visited them earlier that day for lunch, but then she had gone back to work. She had an important job at *Candy Land*, which was a big sweet factory on a hill overlooking Wetherbury.

"Ooh, you're right!" said Kirsty, crunching on the last piece of her cone. "Come on, let's run the rest of the way!"

The girls ran up the street where Kirsty lived and burst in through her front door, panting and giggling.

"Hello, girls!" said Mrs Tate, looking out of the kitchen and smiling at them. "Have you had a nice day?"

"Magical!" said Rachel, thinking of their adventures.

"Kirsty, there's something waiting for you on the dining table," said Mrs Tate.

The girls exchanged excited smiles, then kicked off their shoes and hurried through to the dining table. There they found an envelope propped up against the fruit bowl. It was pink with a lilac trim, and Kirsty's name was written in gold letters on the front.

Eagerly, Kirsty opened the envelope and pulled out two pink cards with sparkly edges. She gasped as she read the words on the cards.

15

"These are tickets for a tour of *Candy Land*," she told Rachel. "Look – there's one for you as well!"

"And the tour is tomorrow!" squealed Rachel. "What a fantastic present!"

"I just hope that we can stop Jack Frost from ruining all the sweets at *Candy Land* – and everywhere else, too," said Kirsty, her face falling slightly.

"If we can't help the rest of the Sweet Fairies to find their magical objects, our tour will be a disaster!"

Baking Blunders

As the girls were gazing at the exciting tickets, Mrs Tate came over and put her arms around their shoulders.

"Girls, would you like to bake some cupcakes for dessert?" she asked.

"Ooh, yes please!" said Kirsty at once.

"We could give some to your Aunt Harri to thank her for the tickets," Rachel suggested.

"That's a great idea," said Kirsty. "I want to make our cupcakes as pretty as the ones at *Cupcake Corner*."

"Isn't that the new shop in the village?" asked Mrs Tate, as she started gathering the ingredients. "They always have delicious-looking cakes in the window."

"Ours are going to be just as yummy," said Rachel.

"You can make the cake mixture on your own," said Mrs Tate. "Call me when you're ready and I'll put the cupcakes in the oven."

She left the kitchen and closed the door behind her. Kirsty looked at the recipe book.

"I'll measure out the flour and sugar while you beat the eggs," she suggested.

Rachel nodded eagerly, but as she picked up the egg box it slipped out of her hand. SMASH! Six eggs lay broken on the kitchen floor, oozing across the tiles.

"Oh no," Rachel groaned. "What a butterfingers!"

"Never mind," said Kirsty. "We've got another box of eggs in the cupboard."

While Kirsty measured out the flour, Rachel cleaned up the mess and fetched the other box of eggs. As she was beating them, Kirsty gave a

squeal and a huge puff of white flour covered both girls.

"Sorry!" Kirsty exclaimed. "I lost my grip on the bag and dumped too much flour into the measuring bowl."

"We're not doing very well, are we?" Rachel laughed, blinking flour out of her eyes and shaking it from her hair. "Never mind, we can just tip it back into the bag."

Soon the cupcake mixture was ready.

"Let's take turns to stir it," said Kirsty. "The recipe says 'stir briskly' – that means fast."

She plunged a wooden spoon into the mixture and stirred hard. Dollops of cake mixture flew everywhere!

"Careful!" cried Rachel. "Here, let me try."

But as soon as she moved the spoon, cake mixture splattered messily into the waiting cupcake cases.

"Hey!" squealed a tiny, bell-like voice.

"That came from inside one of the cupcake cases," said Rachel in astonishment. "Oh, Kirsty, look! That cupcake case is glowing!"

As the girls drew closer, Coco the Cupcake Fairy peered out of the yellow cupcake case, a dollop of cake mix on the tip of her nose.

"Hello, girls," she said. "I wasn't expecting that!"

"Sorry, Coco!" Rachel exclaimed. "We've been trying to make cupcakes, but everything seems to be going wrong."

"No problem," said Coco with a giggle, wiping the cake mixture off the tip of her nose. "Cupcakes are my favourite things – even before they're cooked! I just wish that I had my magical cupcake charm so that I could help to make your cupcakes perfect. I've come to ask you if you'll help me to get it back from Jack Frost and his pesky goblins."

"Of course we will!" Kirsty replied.
"We'll start looking as soon as we've
finished baking."

Just then, Mrs Tate came back into
the kitchen. As quick as a flash, Coco
zoomed into
Rachel's pocket.

"Are the
cupcakes
ready to
go into the
oven?" asked
Mrs Tate.

"Almost,"
said Rachel,
spooning the cake
mixture into the cases.

Kirsty helped her to fill all the cupcake
cases, and then Mrs Tate used her oven

gloves to put the baking tray into the oven.

"Let's make some lovely colourful icing while the cakes are baking," suggested Mrs Tate.

Rachel decided to make some purple icing, and Kirsty chose pink. But as soon as Rachel started to stir the icing mixture, she gave a groan.

"I must have done something wrong," she said. "My icing looks grey!"

"Nothing's going right!" exclaimed Kirsty.

She hurried over to look into Rachel's
bowl, but in her haste her foot slipped
on a blob of icing that had fallen to the
floor.

"WHOOPS!" she squealed as she
skidded across the kitchen.

Rachel held out her arms. Kirsty
clutched on to them and stopped herself
from falling, her heart thudding.

"Thank you, Rachel!" she said,
panting.

At that moment, the oven timer rang.

"Ooh, the cupcakes are ready!" said Rachel in excitement. "We'll just have them without the icing."

Mrs Tate pulled on her oven gloves and opened the oven door. A little bit of black smoke puffed out as she peered inside.

"Oh no!" she exclaimed.

She pulled out the tray of cupcakes and the girls looked at them in dismay. Some were burnt, while others didn't seem to have cooked at all. A couple had spilled out of their cases. They were ruined!

Fairy Spies

"Girls, I think you must have made a mistake with the recipe," said Mrs Tate, coughing as more black smoke came out of the oven.

"What a disaster," Kirsty said in a miserable voice. "I tried to follow the recipe so carefully, but they're nothing like the ones at *Cupcake Corner*."

While Mrs Tate scraped the burnt cake mixture off the cake tray, Rachel pulled Kirsty aside. Her eyes were sparkling with sudden excitement.

"Kirsty, I bet that Jack Frost's greedy goblins are at *Cupcake Corner*," she whispered. "I think they must have Coco's magical charm, and that's why the cupcakes in the shop are so perfect."

Kirsty's eyes opened wide. "You're right!" she said. "But how are we going to stop them?"

32

"I've got an idea," sad Rachel, turning to Kirsty's mum. "Mrs Tate, may we go to *Cupcake Corner* to buy some cupcakes for later, because ours have gone wrong?"

"I think that's a very good idea," said Mrs Tate.

Rachel and Kirsty pulled on their shoes and picked up their purses. Then they hurried out with Coco still safely tucked in Rachel's pocket.

The girls ran all the way to *Cupcake Corner*, hoping that they were right. They stopped by the window and panted to catch their breath, gazing at the display of beautifully iced cupcakes.

"They're so pretty," said Coco, popping her head out of Rachel's pocket. "Look at those red ones that have been arranged to look like a bunch of roses!"

"I like the butterfly shape," said Kirsty, pointing to a large pink-and-white display in the centre of the window.

34

"They all look completely delicious," said Rachel, gazing at a tall stand with tiers of iced cupcakes, each decorated with a tiny candy fairy. "My stomach's rumbling!"

"I wonder why Jack Frost wants *these* cupcakes to be perfect," said Kirsty. "I expect the baker is selling plenty of them!"

"Yes, look," said Rachel, peering past the displays into the shop. "There's a man and lots of children at the counter. I wonder if he's buying some cakes for a party."

Just then, the shortest of the children turned around and pulled a face at the girls. They both gasped. The face was green!

"Those children are goblins!" Kirsty exclaimed.

"And that man is wearing an ice-blue cape," added Rachel. "I bet it's Jack Frost. We have to find out what he's up to!"

"Coco, will you turn us into fairies?" asked Kirsty. "Then we can keep out of sight and hear what they're saying."

"Good idea!" said Coco, fluttering out of Kirsty's pocket.

Luckily there was no one in the street, and the girls ducked down below the window ledge so that the goblins couldn't see them.

Coco balanced on Kirsty's knee, standing on one foot like a ballerina. Her golden-brown hair gleamed and her hair jewels sparkled in the evening sun. She waved her wand in a wide circle and hundreds of tiny, sparkling cupcakes flew from it. They whirled around Rachel and Kirsty, who at once smelled the delicious aroma of baking cakes.

Their skin tingled as the magic began
to work, and they shrank to fairy-size.
Pastel-coloured wings appeared on
their backs and they fluttered them in
excitement, pirouetting into the air.

"Come on, let's go inside," said
Rachel, leading the way into the pretty
shop through a small open window.
They hid behind some cupcakes on the
top tier of a cake stand, and carefully
peered out.

Jack Frost was standing at the counter in his ice-blue cape, talking to the baker. Three goblins were beside him, each of them wearing green shorts and T-shirts decorated with a cupcake pattern. While Jack Frost was talking, they were  sneaking sly nibbles of the cupcakes on display around the shop.

"Look!" Coco whispered. "Even their hats are shaped like cupcakes."

"What is Jack Frost saying?" asked Kirsty. "We have to find out!"

A Rude Customer

"And don't forget to put my face on each cupcake in blue icing," the girls heard Jack Frost snap. "There had better not be a single cupcake without my image on it! Do you hear me?"

"Yes, sir," said the baker, looking surprised at Jack Frost's rudeness. "I will need a picture to copy."

"That's easy," said Jack, pulling a photograph out of his pocket. "I always carry a few pictures of myself around with me. I like to have something handsome to look at sometimes, instead of this ugly lot."

He jerked his thumb at the goblins, and the baker gave a nervous giggle.

"He thinks Jack Frost is joking," Kirsty whispered.

"Are you having a party then, sir?" asked the baker, as he wrote down the order.

"Party?" Jack Frost exclaimed. "Pah!

I'm going to use lots and lots of cupcakes to make a throne. Look, here's my design."

He thrust a crumpled piece of paper under the baker's nose.

"But...but...if you try to sit on the cupcakes you'll simply squash them," said the baker.

"Are you calling me FAT?" roared Jack Frost.

"No, no, sir!" the baker cried, shaking his head. "Now, this is a  very big order so it will take us some time – perhaps you would like to pop back later?"

"We'll wait," Jack Frost growled.

The baker gave him an alarmed look and hurried into the kitchen.

"That stupid baker doesn't know my clever plan," said Jack Frost, rubbing his bony hands together. "When the cupcakes are finished I'll add an ingredient of my own – a magical spell that will make them strong enough to sit on. Then at last I can settle down on a cushion of tasty, soft sponge!"

"It's a brilliant plan!" said the short goblin with a slimy smile.

"You're a genius," said the second goblin, bowing.

But the third goblin didn't say anything flattering at all — he was too busy nibbling a cupcake. Jack Frost saw him, gave a furious yell and grabbed him by the ear.

"Listen to me, gargoyle face," he shouted. "If anyone's going to eat these cupcakes, it's going to be ME!"

With a bolt of icy blue magic he whipped the cake away from the goblin and shoved it into his mouth.

"Now you listen to me!" he shouted, spraying bits of cake all over the cowering goblins. "Find me lots and lots of cupcakes and bring them back to the Candy Castle, OR ELSE! I've got a lot to do, and I have to get going!"

He pulled out a piece of paper and waved it under the goblins' noses. The girls leaned forward and saw, in messy handwriting, the words:

Candy Castle - To Do List

Jack Frost reached inside
his cape and pulled out
something that glimmered
under the lights. It was
small and golden
and shaped like
a cupcake. Coco
gasped and clutched
at Rachel and Kirsty.

"Girls, that's my cupcake charm!" she
whispered.

Jack Frost handed the charm to the
short goblin, who had been pulling faces
at the girls earlier. He held it in both
hands, his eyes opening very wide.

"Thank you for trusting me with this,
Master," he babbled. "I promise that– "

"Shut up!" Jack Frost snapped. "I
haven't got time to listen to your flattery.

Just hurry up and bring me lots of lovely cupcakes – or you'll all be sorry!"

Before the goblins could say another word, he disappeared with a rumble of thunder and a bolt of icy magic.

Two of the goblins immediately turned to the cupcakes and started scoffing them, but the short goblin put his hands on his hips.

"You mustn't do that," he said. "Jack Frost wouldn't like it."

"Yah boo, goody two-shoes!" sneered the first goblin.

"Master's pet!" the second goblin added.

The short goblin tried to grab the cupcakes back, and the three of them started to scuffle.

"We have to get that cupcake charm back!" Rachel whispered to Kirsty and Coco. "Listen, while those goblins are squabbling, maybe we could creep up on them?"

"Let's try it," agreed Coco. "It's dangerous, but I can't bear to see my cupcake charm in that goblin's hand any longer!"

Icing to the Rescue

As quietly as they could, the three fairies tiptoed out from behind the cupcakes and fluttered down to the middle shelf of the cake stand.

"So far, so good," Kirsty whispered. "The goblins are too busy arguing to notice us."

They flew down to the bottom shelf. Still, none of the goblins had noticed them.

"Now for the tricky part," said Rachel.

She led the way across the bakery until they were hovering inches behind the short goblin's hand. He was clutching  Coco's magical cupcake charm tightly, but his attention was on the other goblins. Rachel reached out her hand towards the charm...

Suddenly the first goblin spotted her!
"Fairies!" he yelled.

"Where?" shouted the short goblin.

"Hide!" cried Coco.

The short goblin spun
around and bumped
into a display
table. Cupcakes
tumbled
everywhere.

"Pick
them up!" he
squawked. "We
mustn't damage a
single one!"

By the time the goblins
had picked the cupcakes up, each of the
fairies had landed on top of a cupcake
and posed like a candy decoration.

Rachel, Kirsty and Coco stood as still as they could while the goblins hunted around the shop for them. They looked behind displays and peered up at the ceiling, but they couldn't see the fairies anywhere.

"They must have gone," said the first goblin eventually. "All this searching has made me hungry, though."

He turned to the display table and lifted up the cupcake with Rachel on top. His mouth opened wide, and Rachel gave a gasp of fear. He was about to eat her!

"Quick, Coco!" exclaimed Kirsty, rising into the air. "We have to save Rachel!"

As they zoomed into the air, Rachel darted away from the goblin's mouth, holding her nose against his bad breath. The goblin gave a screech and swatted at her as if she were a fly.

"There they are!" he squawked. "Get them! Stop them!"

Rachel, Kirsty and Coco whizzed and zigzagged around the shop as fast their wings could carry them, dodging the furious goblins. Bakery boxes were flung into the air and cake stands crashed to the floor as the goblins rampaged through the shop. But the short goblin still had the magical charm in his hand, and the fairies were getting out of breath. They had to think of something fast!

Suddenly, Kirsty had an idea.

"Rachel, remember how I slipped on that icing earlier?" she panted. "If Coco can cover the floor in icing, that might stop the goblins from chasing us."

As quick as a flash, Coco waved her wand. Instantly, the floor of *Cupcake Corner* was covered with a thick layer of icing. The goblins slipped and slid across it, waving their arms to try to keep their balance.

"They look just like three very bad skaters!" said Kirsty with a giggle.

"HELP!" squealed the short goblin, as his feet headed in opposite directions.

With a squelchy plop, he landed on his bottom in the icing. The magical cupcake charm flew into the air, and Rachel dived towards it.

"Stop her!" howled the goblin.

The other two goblins leaped towards it, but they cracked their knobbly heads together and crashed to the floor, groaning. Rachel caught the beautiful charm and handed it to Coco. At once, it shrank to fairy-size, and all three fairies breathed a sigh of relief.

Coco waved her wand and the icing on the floor disappeared. The cupcake stands and boxes were tidied up in the twinkling of an eye, and the goblins crossly scrambled to their feet.

"Give us that back!" the short goblin demanded.

"Certainly not," said Coco in a calm voice. "It belongs to me."

"You should stop being so greedy," Rachel declared.

"And tell Jack Frost to stop being greedy too," added Kirsty.

The first goblin clapped his hand to his mouth with a horrified expression.

"What are we going to do about Jack Frost's cupcake throne?" he groaned. "Without the charm, we can't gather enough cupcakes for him!"

The Great Cupcake Sale

Coco gave Rachel and Kirsty a little wink, and then waved her wand. A small cupcake floated through the air towards the goblins, decorated with a tiny throne.

"Jack Frost's never going to fit on that!" exclaimed the short goblin.

"It'll have to do," grumbled the second goblin.

He grabbed the cupcake and they all scurried out of the shop, arguing bitterly about who should be allowed to carry it.

"Time for us to become human again, I think," said Rachel.

They fluttered down behind the shop counter, and Coco turned them back to their normal size.

"I'm so grateful for your help, girls," she said, her eyes shining with happiness. "Now I've got my charm back, I know that cupcakes everywhere will be perfect again."

"We loved helping you," said Kirsty with a beaming smile. "Please tell the other Sweet Fairies that we are always here if they need us."

Coco blew them each a kiss, and then pirouetted and disappeared in a flurry of sparkling fairy dust. At that moment, the baker came out of the kitchen.

"Your cupcakes are all ready, sir," he began, and then stopped when he saw that Jack Frost wasn't in the shop.

"I…er…think he's gone," said Rachel.

"But I've just prepared two hundred cupcakes for him!" the baker groaned. "What a waste! I'll never sell all of them this afternoon – it's nearly closing time."

He looked really upset, and the girls felt sorry for him.

"I've got an idea," said Rachel. "How about having a cupcake sale on the street outside the shop? Everyone will be on their way home from work. We'll help, if you like."

The baker
smiled.
"That's a
wonderful
idea,"
he said.
"Thank
you, girls!
You can
bring the cakes outside once I've set up a
table."

Half an hour later, there was a large
crowd of people outside *Cupcake
Corner*. Rachel and Kirsty couldn't fill
the cake boxes fast enough! Everyone
who was on their way home from work
stopped at the cake sale, and most of
them bought a box of cakes to take
home as a treat.

"This blue frosting is so yummy!" said a grey-haired businessman, filling his briefcase with cakes.

"My family will love these for their pudding tonight," said a window cleaner, popping two cake boxes into her bucket.

By closing time, all the beautifully decorated cakes had sold out.

"I'm sorry, girls, there isn't a single blue cupcake left for you to take home," said the baker. "But there will always be a free cupcake for you at *Cupcake Corner*."

"Thank you!" exclaimed Kirsty. "That was great fun!"

As they walked back to Kirsty's house, the girls talked about the day's adventures.

"I can hardly believe how much has happened today," said Kirsty. "We've helped *three* fairies find their charms!"

"Yes, and we've had gorgeous lollipops and delicious ice creams," Rachel remembered, licking her lips. "It's a shame that we won't have any cupcakes tonight, though."

They reached Kirsty's house and went inside. In the kitchen, their cupcakes were still cooling. But they looked very different from earlier…

"These cupcakes are perfect!" Kirsty said with a gasp. "I don't understand it — I thought we'd ruined them!"

"I think Coco must have visited here on her way back to Fairyland," said Rachel with a little smile. "Look."

She pointed to two of the cupcakes. The words "Thank you" were written on them in sparkly golden icing. Rachel and Kirsty exchanged delighted smiles.

"What lovely cupcakes!" exclaimed Mrs Tate, coming into the kitchen. "*Cupcake Corner* certainly makes perfect cakes! Did you get those to thank Aunt Harri for the tickets to *Candy Land*?"

The girls
glanced at
each other
and then
nodded
happily.
They knew
that Coco had left
the cakes for them, but
they didn't mind if Aunt Harri had them.
After all, they weren't greedy like Jack
Frost and his goblins!

"Are you looking forward to your tour
of *Candy Land* tomorrow?" asked Mrs
Tate as she started to get dinner ready.

"Definitely!" said the girls together.

"We'll have to keep our eyes peeled for
Jack Frost and his goblins, though," said
Rachel as they laid the table.

"Yes, they still have four of the Sweet Fairies' charms," Kirsty agreed, "They're bound to be up to mischief."

"And we're bound to be there to stop them," said Rachel with a grin. "I can't wait for our next adventure!"

Now it's time for Kirsty and Rachel to help...

Clara the Chocolate Fairy

Read on for a sneak peek...

"I'm *so* looking forward to this!' Rachel Walker told her best friend, Kirsty Tate, her voice brimming over with excitement. The two girls were walking up one of the hills that overlooked Wetherbury village. "I've never been to a sweet factory before. I can't wait to see inside *Candy Land*."

"Me, too," Kirsty agreed happily. "Wasn't it kind of Aunt Harri to arrange a tour of the factory for my birthday treat?" Kirsty's aunt worked at *Candy Land* in the cookie department.

"Yes, and it isn't your birthday until

tomorrow, so it's almost like having an *extra* treat!" Rachel pointed out as they climbed higher up the hill. Ahead of them they could see the sweet factory with the big pink-and-white *Candy Land* sign over the wrought-iron gates. "Do you think we might get to try a few sweets while we're on the tour?" Rachel added eagerly.

Kirsty grinned. "I hope so!" she replied. "I'm really looking forward to seeing the chocolates being made. My favourite is the Sticky Toffo Choc – it's gorgeous, sticky toffee covered with yummy chocolate!" But then Kirsty's smile faded. "Remember, though, Rachel," she went on, "some of the sweets might not taste very nice, now that Jack Frost and his goblins have the Sweet Fairies' magic charms."

Rachel nodded solemnly. Yesterday, just after she'd arrived to spend the half-term holiday with Kirsty, their old friend Honey the Sweet Fairy had appeared to whisk the girls off to Fairyland. There the girls had met Honey's helpers, the seven Sweet Fairies who looked after all the delicious, mouth-watering sweets in both Fairyland and the human world.

Rachel and Kirsty were very upset when they discovered that Jack Frost and his goblins had stolen the Sweet Fairies' magical charms. But they couldn't believe it when they found out exactly *why* Jack Frost needed the magical charms...

Read Clara the Chocolate Fairy to find out what adventures are in store for Kirsty and Rachel!

Meet the
Sweet Fairies

Meet the fairies, play games
and get sneak peeks at
the latest books!

There's fairy fun for everyone at

www.rainbowmagicbooks.co.uk

You'll find great activities, competitions, stories and
fairy profiles, and also a special newsletter.

Win Rainbow Magic Goodies!

There are lots of Rainbow Magic fairies, and we want to know which one is your favourite! Send us a picture of her and tell us in thirty words why she is your favourite and why you like Rainbow Magic books. Each month we will put the entries into a draw and select one winner to receive a Rainbow Magic Sparkly T-shirt and Goody Bag!

Send your entry on a postcard to Rainbow Magic Competition, Orchard Books, 338 Euston Road, London NW1 3BH.
Australian readers should email: childrens.books@hachette.com.au
New Zealand readers should write to Rainbow Magic Competition, PO Box 3255, Shortland St, Auckland 1140, NZ.
Don't forget to include your name and address.
Only one entry per child.

Good luck!

Nicki the Holiday Camp Fairy

Rachel and Kirsty have been looking forward to camp, but everything is going wrong. Can they help Nicki fix things, before the whole summer is ruined?

www.rainbowmagicbooks.co.uk